PLANT PARTS
Roots, Stems, and Leaves

Maeve Griffin

REAL LIFE readers™

Rosen Classroom™

New York

Published in 2009 by The Rosen Publishing Group, Inc.
29 East 21st Street, New York, NY 10010

Book Design: Daniel Hosek

Photo Credits: Cover, p. 6 © Brandon Blinkenberg/Shutterstock; p. 4 (top) © Psamtik/Shutterstock; p. 4
(bottom) © Nanka/Shutterstock; p. 5 (top right) © Vladimir Melnik/Shutterstock; p. 5 (bottom) © Els Jooren/
Shutterstock; p. 7 © Wunson/Shutterstock; pp. 8 (pine needles), 12 © Photodisc; p. 8 (other leaves)
© Luchschen/Shutterstock; p. 9 (bottom) © Brenda Arlene Smith/Shutterstock; p. 10 © Stanislav Mikhalev/
Shutterstock; p. 11 (left) © Gatsenko Alexander/Shutterstock; p. 11 (right) © Maxim Tupikov/Shutterstock;
p. 14 (top right) © Rob Marmion/Shutterstock; p. 14 (bottom left) © Elena Elisseeva/Shutterstock; p. 14
(bottom right) © Eugene Buchko/Shutterstock.

ISBN: 978-1-4358-0037-3
6-pack ISBN: 978-1-4358-0038-0

Manufactured in the United States of America

Word Count: 175

CONTENTS

WHERE DO PLANTS GROW?

Plants grow all around the world.

They grow on mountains and in deserts.

Some plants even grow in the ocean!

Plants may look very different.
Some are a strange shape.
Some have beautiful colors.

PLANT ROOTS

All plants have many parts.

Roots are an important plant part.

Most roots grow under the ground.

roots

Roots take in water and **minerals**
that a plant needs to live.
Roots can grow very long.

PLANT LEAVES

Leaves are another plant part.

Leaves use air, light, and water to make food.

Different plants have different kinds of leaves.

air + light + water

↓

plant food

PLANT STEMS

stem

Plants have **stems**.

Stems help leaves reach up for sunlight.

Stems carry water and minerals from the roots
to other plant parts.

Plant stems can be wide or thin.

They can be tall or short.

Which of these plants has a thin stem?

stem

OTHER PLANT PARTS

There are other plant parts, too.

Some plants have flowers.

Flowers make seeds.

Many new plants grow from seeds.

make plant seeds

hold leaves, carry water and minerals to plant parts

make food

FLOWERS

LEAVES

STEMS

PLANT PARTS

ROOTS

SEEDS

take in water and minerals

grow into new plants

PEOPLE NEED PLANT PARTS

Plant parts are important to people.

We eat plant parts such as **fruits** and **vegetables**.

We use some plant parts to make buildings, too!

GLOSSARY

fruit (FROOT) A part of a plant eaten for food. Most fruit is sweet.

leaf (LEEF) A flat, often green part of a plant that makes its food.

mineral (MIHN-ruhl) Something that is not an animal, a plant, or another living thing.

root (ROOT) A plant part that grows mostly under the ground.

stem (STEHM) A plant part that holds leaves and flowers.

vegetable (VEHJ-tuh-buhl) A part of a plant eaten for food.

INDEX